To Julie
Love Mom.
6-27-95

PIGWIG

John Dyke

METHUEN

NEW YORK · TORONTO · LONDON · SYDNEY

Published in the United States 1978 by
Methuen Inc.
777 Third Avenue, New York, N.Y. 10017
Library of Congress Catalog Card Number 78–55–390
and simultaneously published in Canada by
Methuen Publications
2330 Midland Avenue, Agincourt, Ontario MIS1P7
ISBN 0–458–93510–7

A *Webb & Bower* Book
Edited, designed and produced by
Webb & Bower Limited, Exeter, England

Printed in Great Britain by
W. S. Cowell Ltd, Ipswich

One spring day a young pig sat sadly under a tree.
His name was Pigwig, and he lived with lots of other animals
on Mr. Brown's farm.

Pigwig was sad because he was in love.
He couldn't sleep, even on his nice clean bed of straw.

The meals that Mr. Brown gave the animals were the very best.
But Pigwig wasn't hungry, he just looked at his food and sat about.

Pigwig was in love with proud Matilda,
but she didn't seem to notice him at all.

Whenever Matilda passed by, Pigwig
turned a deeper shade of pink.
Sometimes he would try to speak,
but he could only stutter.

One day, he plucked up his courage and
said, "I love you, Matilda. Will you be mine?"

"No!" she answered. "I could never
marry a stick-in-the-mud like you. Besides,
you are very plain and very dull."

Pigwig was so ashamed that he didn't eat
his lunch, or drink his tea.

"Oh, how can I ever make her love me?" thought Pigwig,
as Matilda walked past with her elegant nose
in the air. She didn't seem to see him at all.

But no matter how Matilda treated him Pigwig loved her all the more.

Pigwig tried to cheer himself up with a book that he'd found.
In it were pictures of people wearing lovely clothes.
Pigwig thought that these people looked very smart,
not a bit plain and not a bit dull.
He tried to imagine himself wearing nice clothes.

Then he found some pictures of hats.

"If I had a smart hat to wear," thought Pigwig,
"I'm sure that Matilda would love me."

Party hat

Fur hat

Cavalier hat

Sailor's hat

diver's hat

maharajah's hat

brave's hat

bowler hat

French hat

Jesting hat

Shady hat

School hat

detective's hat

very old hat

pointed hat

soft hat

Fez hat

diplomatic hat

brave hat

Jockey's hat

Top hat

Tam o'shanter

magical hat

farmer's hat

clever hat

another brave hat

boating hat

smart hat

Pirate's hat

"Why, I will make myself a hat! I will make
a grand hat that will look just right.
When Matilda sees me in my grand hat, she will see
that I am not a bit plain and not a bit dull,
and she will love me after all."

When the hat was finished, the other animals all said
that it did look grand, so Pigwig went off to show Matilda
and ask her again to be his wife.

"I love you, Matilda. Will you be mine?"

But Matilda only laughed, and said, "No, Mr. Pigwig.
Your hat is too big. I will not marry you in that!
Why, a haystack would make a much better hat!"

So sadly Pigwig threw away his grand hat.

That night Pigwig set to work with scissors and glue
to make a hat like a haystack.
He cut and snipped all night long
while the owl hooted down by the barn.
By breakfast time the hat was finished,
so Pigwig went off again to show Matilda.

"I love you, Matilda. Will you be mine?"

"Oh no!" squealed Matilda.

"Hee hee, Mr. Pigwig, hee hee!
Please go away, go away do.
For your hat's not so big,
that's perfectly true,
but it's very, very tickly."

So Pigwig threw away his haystack hat
and went sadly home.

Next he saw a man on a motorcycle,
wearing a splendid crash helmet.

"Where can I get a hat like that?" he asked.

"At the garage down the road," the man replied.

Pigwig had no money, so he filled a sack with turnips
to pay for the hat, and set off for the garage.

The man at the garage had no hats
in Pigwig's size.

"But if you wait here awhile, I will make you one
from all the bits and pieces lying around," he said.

"Beep, beep, toot, toot," Pigwig said to his friends.
"Look how my new hat shines! Don't you think
that I look fine?" And they all agreed that
he looked very smart, not a bit plain
and not a bit dull.

So, once more Pigwig went to Matilda
to ask her to be his wife.

"I love you, Matilda. Will you be mine?"

But Matilda answered,
"Pigwig, you're a dilly,
you are oh so silly
to wear such a noisy hat.
And that's flat.

"I'm afraid you're trying to tease me,
it simply doesn't please me
to be noisily awakened
by the creaking and the clanking of your hat."

So Pigwig went sadly away to look for a better hat, a hat
that would make Matilda love him.

He went to a rummage sale in the church hall,
to see if he could find one there.

Inside, a jolly lady gave him a cup of tea and a cherry cake.

Then he won a trumpet in the grab bag.

And then he saw a hat table, where he found just what he had been looking for

Pigwig waved goodbye to the kind people at the rummage sale,
and he set off home with his trumpet and new hat.
This time, he felt sure that Matilda would love him.

It was a long way back to the farm and soon it began
to get dark. Pigwig was tired now and was glad
to find a pile of straw by the roadside. He lay down
and soon fell asleep, still wearing his hat
and holding his trumpet tightly in his hoof.

That night, while Pigwig slept, a robber broke into Mr. Brown's farm.

He tied everyone up and gagged them,
so they couldn't shout for help.

Then he started to put Mr. Brown's
treasure into his bag.
He took money, jewels, candlesticks
and silver. He was very busy!

Meanwhile, Pigwig left his road-side bed
and set out again for the farm. His hat was tilted,
a bit squashed, but still tight about his head.

It was nearly light when Pigwig
reached the farm. He knew at once
that something was wrong. It was
too quiet and he could see the flicker
of a flash-light in the kitchen.

Tiptoeing to the window, he
peeped inside. Pigwig saw the
robber putting things into his
bag. "I must give the alarm" he
thought excitedly; and he blew a
loud Ta Ra Ra! on his trumpet.

The robber jumped at the sound. He turned round
and saw through the window a shape that shocked him.
It was only the shadow of Pigwig and his hat,
but the robber didn't know that.

With a terrified scream he dropped his bag and began to run.
But he tripped and fell with a heavy crash.

Pigwig wasted no time. Like the really brave pig
that he was, he rushed to the robber and sat on him,
making it impossible for him to escape.

Then Pigwig blew loudly on his trumpet to fetch help. Soon, a policeman came and the robber was marched off to jail.

Everyone heard of Pigwig's brave deed.
All kinds of nice things were written about him.
The newspapers said: HEROIC DEED BY LOCAL PIG

Pigwig was now a great hero and Matilda was proud of him.
It was clear that he was a very fine pig,
not a bit plain and not a bit dull.

Pigwig decided to ask Matilda one last time to be his wife.

"Matilda, I love you. Will you be mine?"

And because she knew that she did love him too,
Matilda said, "Yes."

And Pigwig became the happiest animal in the world.